MAVIS AND MERNA

Ian Wallace

A GROUNDWOOD BOOK

DOUGLAS & McINTYRE   TORONTO   VANCOUVER   BERKELEY

Groundwood Books / Douglas & McIntyre
720 Bathurst Street, Suite 500, Toronto, Ontario M5S 2R4
Distributed in the USA by Publishers Group West
1700 Fourth Street, Berkeley, CA 94710

We acknowledge for their financial support of our publishing program the Canada Council for the Arts, the Government of Canada through the Book Publishing Industry Development Program (BPIDP) and the Ontario Arts Council.

ONTARIO ARTS COUNCIL
CONSEIL DES ARTS DE L'ONTARIO

Library and Archives Canada Cataloguing in Publication
Wallace, Ian
Mavis and Merna / Ian Wallace.
ISBN 0-88899-647-0
I. Title.
PS8595.A566M39 2005   jC813'.54   C2004-904831-7

Printed and bound in China

The illustrations are done in watercolor on Arches paper.

For my friends, Barbara and John,
who took me to Gully's.
And to Annie Morgan who greeted us.

GULLY'S was the busiest store in Fortune's Cove. It sold everything a family could ever need. Bicycles and birdbaths. Church hats and long johns. Cream of Wheat and canoes. Hammers and licorice whips. And fish clocks that marked time with their tails.

Mavis loved the store with its tinkling bell above the front door. She loved the smell of wicker and wool, rubber and oil, perfume and leather all mixed up together. She even loved just standing in the aisles imagining owning such wonderful things.

One Halloween night, Mavis had just put on the witch's costume she'd bought at Gully's store when a neighbor, Mr. Quirk, opened the front door. "Joe Gully's dead," he said. "His heart stopped and he dropped like a rock while making his nightly deposit at the bank."

"I'll bet Mrs. Gully's really sad," Mavis sighed.

Her mother looked down at her crystal ball. "Joe's money will help her feel better. Merna will be the merriest widow of them all."

Joe Gully was laid out in the main aisle of his store between the boots and brassieres for three days. Everyone in town came to pay their respects. Mavis didn't hear the tinkling bell when she stepped through the front door. The ringer had been taped so it wouldn't make a sound. The silence made her sad.

"That coffin was a solid gold Cadillac," her father said on the cold walk home. "Joe Gully will look like Elvis Presley riding up to the Pearly Gates in that shiny honker."

"Merna must have picked it out," her mother said. "If Joe had had his way he'd have been buried in a cardboard box."

"I'll bet store prices will really fall now with Merna in charge," said her father.

Mavis thought her parents were being awful, but still her eyes lit up. She hadn't imagined the possibility of dropping prices. Visions of things that she wanted made her giddy.

The next morning, she went to Gully's, but the lights were out and the
door was locked. She sat on a bench and waited for the store to open.
But Mrs. Gully didn't appear that day or any day for the next month.
"Mrs. Gully must be really lonely," Mavis told her parents.

"As lonely as a woman can be counting her millions," replied her mother.

"Merna Gully doesn't have to work another day in her life," said her father.

Mavis wondered, How could anyone have that much money?

That night Mavis sneaked out her bedroom window. She raced across
town to the large Gully house. She crept onto the porch and peered in the
living-room window. There wasn't even one penny lying on the carpet.
She checked out every window on the first floor. Not a cent in any of
those rooms either.

She looked at the tall oak tree on the north side of the house. Then up she climbed until she could see through the windows on the second floor.

"There's not a penny anywhere!"

A twig snapped and the branches swayed in the wind. Mavis spotted Mrs. Gully in the turret room. She wasn't counting money. She was playing Solitaire.

Mavis inched forward and the branch bent beneath her weight.
Suddenly, she lost her balance and crashed down on the front porch roof.
Mrs. Gully threw open the window. "Mavis Cave, come in here! What
a scare you gave me. Are you trying to kill us both?"

Mavis rubbed her elbows. "No. I came to see if you're okay."
"In a tree at ten fifteen? Do your parents know where you are?"
"No," admitted Mavis.

Mavis climbed into the turret room. She brought Mrs. Gully a glass of water from the bathroom. There wasn't any money anywhere. "I loved your store. And everything in it."

Tears welled in Mrs. Gully's eyes. "Joe would have liked that."

"I love Solitaire, too," Mavis said. Mrs. Gully's face lit up.

They played seven games of Double Solitaire. Mavis beat the pants off Mrs. Gully. She won every game before leaving for home by the front door just around midnight.

"Let's do this again, Mavis," Mrs. Gully said. "But tell your parents first."

At breakfast the next morning, Mavis's mother said, "As long as you're keeping the Merry Widow company, I guess it's all right. But please use the front door."

Mavis kept her promise. Through the long bleak winter months Mavis and Merna played Double Solitaire for Pot of Gold chocolates while snacking on pretzels and gingersnaps gobbled down with peppermint ice cream.

"I never get to eat these things at home," Mavis said.

They always sat in the turret room where they could look over the town and the sea. Mavis sat in Mr. Gully's chair. They always lost track of the time.

"Did you know when my dad shovels snow he always piles it on the right?"

"Have you noticed that Mr. Quirk delivers the mail along the exact same route every day?"

"Did you know my mom does laundry only on Fridays?"

"BORING," they snorted and broke into fits of laughter.

When spring came, Mavis showed Mrs. Gully how to work the
lawnmower.

"Joe always cut the grass," Mrs. Gully said. "He wouldn't pay
someone to do it as long as he had a strong heart and two good legs."

Mrs. Gully didn't like mowing in straight lines. "They're too rigid." So they walked in wavy lines, circles and zigzags. "Don't you think the grass looks more jazzy this way?" she asked.

Mavis agreed.

When their yard work was done, they went fishing, or digging for clams when the tide was out. "I haven't done this since I was a girl," Mrs. Gully said.

"Then you are long overdue," Mavis replied.
They always built a fire and waited for the lobster boats to come back from sea.

That summer Mrs. Gully learned to drive her husband's car, a black '58 Chevy Impala newly painted a fiery red. Mavis learned to read maps and navigated as they drove down roads they'd never traveled before. They smoked licorice cigars while sipping root beer through straws and sang along with the rock and roll songs on the radio.

"I know cigars are bad for you and root beer rots your teeth, but we're cruising the open road and who cares!" Mrs. Gully would chortle.

Once, Mavis asked Mrs. Gully why she hadn't opened the store again.

"I was tired of selling boots and brassieres," she replied. "And it wouldn't be the same without the sound of Joe's shoes squeaking across the floor."

Three decades passed. Mavis grew up. Mrs. Gully shrank three inches.

Mavis married a lobster fisherman named Todd and worked alongside him on their boat, *Gully's Float*. Mrs. Gully gave it to them for a wedding present. "In payment for countless mowed lawns and for the pleasure of countless clams shucked," she said.

Sometimes Mrs. Gully joined them at sea.

On Saturday nights they played Triple Solitaire for Pot of Gold chocolates while snacking on pretzels and gingersnaps gobbled down with peppermint ice cream. They always sat in the turret room.

Mavis's parents went to Florida for the winter so her father wouldn't have to shovel snow. Her mother bought a clothes dryer and used it only on Fridays. Mr. Quirk still delivered the mail taking the exact same route every day.

One afternoon, Mavis went to play Double Solitaire. Mrs. Gully was waiting. She was dangling a brass key on a string.

"It's time," she said. "It's long overdue." Mavis knew immediately what she meant.

They drove downtown and unlocked the door to Gully's Store. Mrs. Gully turned on the lights, then removed the tape from the bell.

The bell tinkled, and once again the smell of wicker and wool, rubber and oil, perfume and leather all mixed together. They walked up and down the aisles they hadn't walked in thirty years. The boxes, bags and tins still bore the original prices.

"Everything's an antique now," said Mavis.

"Like me," laughed Mrs. Gully. "Only dustier."

They cleaned everything up then opened the store a week later, leaving the original prices on every item. Mrs. Gully didn't see any reason to change them. Now, anyone coming through the front door would hear the tinkling bell and be able to buy something from 1965. Something they had always wanted, but maybe couldn't afford back then.

"Everything's on sale now," Mrs. Gully said, and she and Mavis laughed so hard they fell into a bin of socks. And they both knew that at the exact moment, Mr. Gully was rolling around in his honking big, solid gold Cadillac.